D0571495

WITHDRAWN

THE DANGER JOE SHOW
Growling Grizzly

by Jon Buller and Susan Schade

SCHOLASTIC INC.
New York   Toronto   London   Auckland   Sydney
Mexico City   New Delhi   Hong Kong   Buenos Aires

Visit Jon Buller and Susan Schade at their website: www.bullersooz.com

ISBN 0-439-40140-2

12 11 10 9 8 7 6 5 4 3 2   2 3 4 5 6 7/0

Printed in the U.S.A.   40

First Scholastic paperback printing, June 2002

For Danger Joe Denham—
the original

electron
(—)

proton
(+)

CHAPTER ONE
DANGER JOE, JR.

It's Monday morning.

I'm standing in front of the whole class. Everybody is looking at me.

The VCR is set up. And they're all waiting for me to show my video.

That rotten Edgar Pitts has a smirky look on his face.

But I'm not worried.

I can stare him down any day. I squint my eyes at him.

Edgar Pitts has spiky hair. I think he puts gel in it.

Here's what I know about Edgar Pitts: He doesn't like me.

Here's how I know he doesn't like me: In kindergarten, my dad brought some snakes to our class. (My dad is DANGER JOE DENIM. He has a show on TV about wild animals. You might have seen it.)

One of Dad's snakes was a big bull snake named Bob. Everybody got to touch Bob. Except Edgar Pitts. He had to go to the bathroom.

After Dad left, Edgar Pitts came up to me and poked me in the chest.

"Who do you think you are?" he asked. "DANGER JOE, JUNIOR? Ha-ha-ha!"

"No, I'm just Joe, Jr.," I said. "It's my *dad* who is Danger Joe."

"Show-off!" he said. "Well, I'm not scared of your dad's old snakes. And I Don't Like You!"

And he hasn't liked me ever since. Well, I don't like him, either!

I quit trying to stare down Edgar Pitts. Who cares, anyway? Instead, I look at my two best friends in the world, Bernie and Kay. The three of us always sit together at lunch.

Kay smiles and Bernie gives me a thumbs-up sign. They don't know the bad news about my video. Yet.

Here's how the video thing is supposed to work:

Every kid in our class gets to take the school camcorder home for one weekend. You make a video and bring it in on Monday. It's a fun kind of homework.

So last weekend, it was my turn. I took the school camcorder home on Friday afternoon.

The only trouble is, now it's Monday, and I don't have my video. And that's not the worst of it.

Mrs. Wright, our teacher, is staring at me. She says, "We're all waiting, Joe."

I say, "Oh," and I look at the floor and shuffle my feet around. My cheeks feel kind of hot. I think maybe I should have stayed home sick today.

"The thing is, I don't have a video," I finally say.

Mrs. Wright's eyebrows shoot up an inch or two.

"And not only that," I add, "the school camcorder got, uh . . . kinda wrecked."

There is a big gasp from everyone. Except Edgar Pitts. He is smiling.

I knew this would happen.

The kids are all whispering and glaring. Now *everybody* hates me. Not just Edgar Pitts.

Probably even Mrs. Wright hates me.

"But wait!" I say. "I can explain!"

CHAPTER TWO
THE RATTLESNAKE

Last Friday, I got off the school bus with my book bag and the school camcorder.

We have a long dirt driveway.

I'm walking toward our house and thinking, *I'm gonna make a great video! I'll get my dad to help me. Wait until the kids see it!* I'm not expecting to have any trouble with my video. What could possibly go wrong?

"JOEY! HEY, JOEY! LOOK WHAT I FINDED!"

It's my round-headed little sister, Jane, in her dusty overalls. She's dragging a pink pillowcase along the ground.

"What have you got?" I ask.

She holds the pillowcase open, and I look inside. Down in the bottom there's a small brownish snake, all curled up. It's looking right at me. It sticks out its tongue and rattles its tail.

"Yow!" I yell. I jump back. I look again.

"Janie, that's a *rattlesnake*! It's *very venomous*!" I cry.

She says, "Isn't he cute? He's a baby."

"Don't you know what venomous means?" I say. "It means poisonous! You can't play with poisonous snakes! Even baby ones are dangerous. You have to learn to be more careful! A rattlesnake has poison in its fangs. What if it bit you?!"

Jane is never careful. I don't know why she hasn't been bitten a million times already.

"I know what veminous is!" she says. "And I was *too* careful! I catched him with Daddy's snake stick."

"Caught," I say. "You *caught* him."

"That's what I said."

"Give me that bag!" I say, grabbing for it. "You're too little to play with poisonous snakes!"

"Ma!" yells Jane, running up the driveway with her dirty pillowcase.

My mother comes out of the house. She's still wearing her work clothes from the bank. She looks nice. "What is it this time?" she asks.

"Joey's trying to get my rattler!" says Jane.

My mother looks at the pink pillowcase and all the color goes out of her face. "Rattler?" she says in a weak voice. She steadies herself against the fence.

"See!?" I say to Jane.

I turn to Mom. "You didn't let me play with snakes until I was in second grade," I complain. "She doesn't know anything! She shouldn't be allowed!"

"I do too know!" says Jane. "I know a lot! I know my rattler is just a baby because he has only three rattles on his tail."

"That isn't quite true," I say. "He's got two

rattles and a button. And he gets a new rattle every time he sheds his skin, so . . ."

"I know!" says Miss Smarty-pants. "So he's just a baby. Less than one year old. You can ask Daddy if you don't believe me! I learned it from his show."

My mother has recovered from her snake shock. She holds out her hand. "Give me that pillowcase, Jane. And watch out! Even a baby rattler can bite you through the cloth."

Jane sticks out her lip.

"Right now!" Mom orders.

Jane hands over the pillowcase. Mom holds it with her arm straight out. "Honestly, Jane, you and your father are like two peas in a pod! No common sense at all!" Mom gives Jane a hug with her free arm. "From now on, you are not to touch *any* snakes. Understand? You could have been seriously hurt!"

She takes the bag over to an empty garbage can, drops it in, and puts the lid on.

"Yow!" howls Jane. Her eyes are wide with horror. "You throwed him away!"

"I'm not throwing the snake away, Jane," my mother says. "I'm just putting him in a safe place until Daddy gets here." Then Mom sits on the trash can lid. "OK, Mr. Snake," she says, "you can stay in there for a bit."

"Mom, the snake can't hear you," Jane complains. "He doesn't have ears."

I'm about to explain to Jane that snakes have ears that are *inside* their heads, but then I hear the back door screen. *Slam!*

"Yoo-hoo! Where is everybody?"

That's my dad! Now everything will be OK.

CHAPTER THREE
BRAINSTORMING

Everybody is talking at once.

"Daddy! Mommy throwed out my snake!"

"Dad! Tell Janie she's too little!"

"Joe, you must teach your daughter to be more careful!"

Dad looks in the garbage can and takes out the pink pillowcase.

"Aha!" he says, holding the rattler by the tail. "What have we here? It's a nice, healthy, young rattlesnake. Whoa, he's a fierce little guy, isn't he? I think it's time to let him go now, Jane."

"Not by the house!" cries my mother.

"Don't worry, Linda," Dad says to her. "We'll take him in the car. I know a place where there are no houses and not too many other snakes. He'll be happier there."

"Can't we keep him in one of your reptile tanks, Daddy?" Jane says.

"No, Jane. The tanks are only for injured animals that we've rescued," Dad explains. "When the animals are healthy, we always put them back into their natural habitat. Their habitat is the place where they live in nature. It has everything the animals need, and it's where they want to be. You know that."

"But Daddy, I *like* him!"

"If you like him, you'll let him go. Besides, I don't think *he* likes *you*."

"He doesn't?" Jane says in a small voice.

I feel kind of sorry for Jane. I always want the animals to like me, too.

I just hope Dad tells her she's too little to play with poisonous snakes. He's read tons of books, and it's taken him years to learn how to hold a snake. He's a real professional. That's why he always says, "DON'T TRY THIS IN YOUR OWN BACKYARD!" That's good advice. He should tell it to Jane!

Then I remember my video. I wonder if I should have been filming the rattler.

Nah. It was pretty small. And that pink pillowcase looked silly. I want my video to be cool. And exciting!

Mom and I change into our after-school clothes, and I grab something to eat. Then I go out to the backyard and take a look at Dad's reptile tanks.

One tank has an iguana in it. The other has a black racer snake with a strange lump. I'm not allowed to touch the sick reptiles. Once they get better, Dad will find a way to release them back into the wild.

Soon Dad and Jane come back with the empty pillowcase. Jane sees the cookies in my hand.

"Hey!" she says. "Where'd you get those?"

"From Mom," I say.

Jane runs off to find Mom. And cookies. Good.

I tell Dad about the video I have to make for school.

"Do you think you can help me come up with some good ideas for it?" I ask.

"Sure," he says. He squats down next to the turtle tank. "We should be able to think of some good ideas if we work together. We'll brainstorm."

"OK!" I squat down, too.

Dad picks up one of the turtles. "Want to film Looie?" he says.

Looie is a rescued painted turtle with a missing foot.

"Smile, Looie," Dad says. He touches Looie on the head, and Looie opens his mouth.

Looie isn't very exciting.

"Hey!" I say. "We could go hiking and find an animal in its natural habitat!" (I know that Dad

is big on natural habitats.) "Like a mountain lion! That would be so cool! Maybe we could even find a mountain lion with cubs. I could film the cubs playing. And the mother hunting for food!"

I stop and think about that. "Except not the killing part," I add. (I know killing is natural for mountain lions. It's how they eat. But I don't like it. And I don't want it in my video.)

Dad sets Looie back in his tank.

"You know, Joe, Jr.," he says to me, "it's not that easy to find mountain lions. They're very secretive animals."

Rats.

"I'll tell you what," he continues, "I have to fly to the Mosquito Mountains this weekend. My buddy, Ranger Wally, has been watching a colony of hoary marmots for me. We'll be shooting some scenes for my hoary marmot show. Would you like to come along?"

Would I?!

Now, I know that hoary marmots are just big woodchucks. But I'm sure something more exciting will come along. How can I be so sure? Because there's always danger when my dad is filming his show! That's why they call him DANGER JOE!

CHAPTER FOUR
ALL ABOUT BEAR COUNTRY

It's Saturday morning, early, and Dad and I are packing our backpacks. Jane is still asleep.

I check my list:

water bottle
sleeping pad
sleeping bag
rain gear
toothbrush
extra socks
compass
pocket flashlight

binoculars
waterproof matches
freeze-dried food
insect repellent
Swiss army knife
litter bags
fish hook and string
identification

You always have to take extra food with you in case you get lost or stranded. Freeze-dried food is the best because it won't go bad and it's light to carry. It doesn't smell much, either, so it won't attract animals. You just mix it with water before you eat it. It's like what the astronauts have in space, but it doesn't taste that great.

My mom is following my dad around the house.

For some reason, she always worries when we go camping.

"Do you think he's old enough, Joe?" she says to my dad. "You won't let him out of your sight, will you? Not even when you're working with the animals?"

(I guess she knows my dad pretty well. He can get distracted when he's around animals.)

"Have you got the first aid kit?" she asks him. "And the cell phone? And your money belt?"

"We're only filming hoary marmots, Linda," Dad says. "We'll be fine."

"Yes, but we both know that there are much bigger animals than marmots in the Mosquito Mountains."

"I'll be on the lookout," Dad replies. "Joe, Jr., won't be in any danger."

Of course, when we get in the car, it's another story.

"Okay, son," Dad says once we've buckled our seat belts. "We're heading into bear country, where you can never be completely safe. But don't worry. *I'll* be there."

(I know. But it's *him* I'm worried about! My dad is a danger magnet.)

We turn left onto the main road. Dad is saying, "Now, just in case you do run into bear trouble, let me give you some tips."

And I'm thinking, *A bear might be a good subject for my video!*

"The best thing," Dad says, "is for bears and people to stay away from each other. You should always let a bear know you're coming. That gives him a chance to get out of your way. You should also make a lot of noise and keep *upwind* of him. Upwind is when the wind is blowing your scent his way, so he can smell you. If he can smell you, he can get out of your way."

"I know what upwind is, Dad," I say. "But what if I want to see a bear?"

"Well, son, bears are extremely dangerous. You should always try to avoid bears — that's your best bet."

I'm looking out the window. "You just went by the doughnut shop," I say.

"Whoops!" Dad makes a U-turn and we go back for doughnuts. We always stop for doughnuts on the way to the airfield.

After I finish my doughnut, I say, "If I do see a bear, is it true that I should climb a tree to get away from it?"

"A tree is good. But only if the bear is a grizzly. Grizzly bears have large humps behind their necks and very long claws. They aren't good at climbing. But other bears, like black bears, can be excellent climbers. And they're all fast runners. You shouldn't run from bears. They can run faster than you."

"They can?! I didn't know that!"

"Yep. A lot faster. And you never know what they'll do. That's why they're so dangerous. It's hard to know how to protect yourself."

OK, I'm starting to get the picture.

"Anyway," Dad continues, "the best advice I can give you is to . . ."

I know what he's going to say. "THINK LIKE A GRIZZLY!" I shout. That is one of Dad's favorite things to say on his show. He always wants people to think like animals.

Just then we pull up to the floatplane dock. We meet Dad's producer, Lucy. She's the one who's in charge of organizing the show. And the cameraperson, Elton. They both know me already.

There are six floatplanes lined up at the edge of the water. We load all the gear into one of them and board the plane. Then Jim, the pilot, takes off.

We're headed for Diamond Lake, high in the Mosquito Mountains!

I can't wait! My video is gonna be so cool.

CHAPTER FIVE
THE JUNIOR RANGERS

We fly to the mountains. Down below, we can see tiny cars snaking up the Zigzag Highway. Then we don't see anybody anymore. Just miles and miles of wilderness.

I can tell when we get to Diamond Lake.

One wingtip dips down, and we make a wide circle over this lake that's all sparkly, like diamonds.

The pontoons of the floatplane touch down, and we skim along the surface of the water. Right up to the shore.

Elton, the cameraperson, steps out too soon and gets water in his boots.

I wave good-bye to Jim. He will be back on

Sunday afternoon to pick us up. That means I have two whole days to make my video.

Well, a day and a half.

Dad's buddy, Ranger Wally, is waiting for us. He helps us carry our gear to the campsite. It's a small clearing in the forest, beside the trail. You can see Diamond Lake through the trees.

There's a metal box for the food. That's so we don't attract bears.

It's bad to feed people food to bears. If you do, they'll start to want food from people all the time. That could lead to trouble — for the people and the bears. Feeding bears human food is one of the worst things you can do.

Speaking of human food, it's time for lunch.

Ranger Wally rubs his hands together. He knows we've brought some *real* sandwiches. (Wally has been camping up here for a long time and living on canned stew and freeze-dried eggs.)

Elton sets up a camp chair in front of his

tent. He takes off his soaked boots and hangs his socks on a bush to dry.

"I know they won't dry in time!" he says, walking around carefully in his bare feet. "And I'll probably get blisters! *And* catch a chill. That's all I need! I don't know why we couldn't have come by helicopter! At least we could have landed on dry ground!"

"Didn't you bring extra socks?" I say. "I always bring extra socks."

"You would," says Elton. Elton is from New York City. He isn't very good at roughing it.

Elton unwraps his sandwich. It's a large pastrami sub.

"Make sure you burn that wrapping," says Dad. "Whew! I can smell it all the way over here."

"No way!" says Elton. "I need it to rewrap! I'm saving half my sub for tomorrow! I can't eat that freeze-dried glop!"

"Sorry," says Ranger Wally, "but do you

know how good a bear's sense of smell is? A bear can smell food from miles away! And by the way, I wouldn't let that pastrami drip on my clothes if I were you."

"Yaaah!" yelps Elton, mopping at the slop on his shirt.

Because Elton can't eat a whole large sub in one sitting, Ranger Wally gets to finish it. "Man, this tastes good!" he says.

"Phooey," says Elton.

"So you came along to look after your dad?" Lucy, the producer, asks me. She knows that Dad can get into trouble sometimes.

I tell her about the video I have to make for school.

"Cool," she says. "Just be careful not to get in Elton's way when he's filming your dad."

"OK," I say. I'm not having any people in my video, anyway. Just animals.

Jingle, jingle. We hear the sound of little bells.

"Hey, what's that?" says Elton. "It sounds like Santa's reindeer!"

"I know what it is," I say. "It's some hikers wearing bear bells, to warn bears that they're coming. That way the bears won't be taken by surprise and attack them. I just wish they weren't coming here. They might scare all *our* animals away!"

"Well, they've sure scared Danger Joe," laughs Elton. "He just scooted into his tent like a rabbit!"

"*Nothing* scares Danger Joe!" I say.

Lucy explains it to Elton. "We just don't want any fans around, getting in the way of the filming and spooking the animals. If they see Danger Joe, it's all over! We'll never get any work done."

Jingle, jingle. A whole bunch of girls come tramping up the trail, wearing huge backpacks. I count eight girls and two grown-ups. The girls look about my age. Or a little older.

They stop and talk to us.

"Wow!" one says. "Look at all the camera stuff! Are you guys making a movie?"

"Just doing some research," Ranger Wally says. "But I'm going to have to ask you to take the other trail. This one is off-limits today, and tomorrow, too." He shows them his badge.

"Oh! But we're from the Junior Rangers Club, and we wanted to see Pig Tail Peak!" one of their leaders says.

"No problem," Ranger Wally says. He unfolds his pocket map. "See this trail? That will get you to Pig Tail, too. And it's easier walking!" He sort of pushes them toward the other trail.

You can tell they don't like it. One of the leaders looks annoyed. The girls keep looking back at us. A girl with brown hair and big eyes stays behind and talks to me.

"So, what are you guys researching?" she asks me.

Uh-oh. What should I say? I'm not very good at lying.

"Just, um, checking some scat samples," I answer.

It's the only thing I can think of at the spur of the moment.

"You know, scat is the word for animal droppings, or . . . poo."

I can feel my face getting red. Oh, jeez! Why did I have to say that?

"Excuse me!" she says, putting her hands on

her hips. "We're Junior Rangers. We know what scat samples are."

Then she trots off after the others.

"I don't think they're researchers at all!" another girl declares in a loud voice. "You don't need all those cameras just to collect scat samples!"

"I'll bet they *are* making a movie!" her friend says. "Do you think that kid is an actor, Iris?"

Iris is the girl who spoke to me. She shrugs.

"Maybe," she says. "Only I don't know what kind of movie they would be making up here in the mountains."

"Maybe it's an animal movie. Like *Doctor Dolittle*!"

"You mean *Doctor* Poo-*little*!"

The group breaks into giggles.

Very funny.

CHAPTER SIX
ON THE TRAIL

When the girls are gone, Danger Joe comes out of his tent. "*Whew!* That was a close one," he says.

Ranger Wally puts up a "TRAIL CLOSED" sign. Then we pull on our day packs and start our hike to the place where the hoary marmots live.

At first, we're walking under tall cedar trees. It's quiet and cool and damp. The ground is covered with moss and ferns.

Ranger Wally leads the way.

Behind him, Lucy is talking to Danger Joe. "So, Joe," she says, "do you think we can get some

shots of hoary marmot babies? Nothing sells like baby animals! I'd really like at least thirty seconds of the babies playing in the meadow."

"I'd like to see babies, too, Lucy, but it might be too early in the season for them to come out of their burrows."

Then he stops short. "Shhhh! Hear that?"

We all stop.

"Fweeee! Fweee!" Danger Joe tries to imitate the sound. "It's the song of the varied thrush! Look! There she is! A female. What a little beauty! Good golly! Isn't nature amazing?"

My dad stops for a while to watch the bird. Lucy finally drags him away.

The forest changes the higher we hike. Now it's mostly spruce trees and fir trees, and it's not so damp.

Elton is wearing borrowed socks.

I can hear him huffing and grumbling behind me. "Why does your father have to have such big feet?" he says. *Huff, huff.* "These socks are all bunching up. If I don't have a blister tonight it will be a miracle!"

I ignore him.

"Darn bugs!" he says. *Swat! Swat!*

When we come out of the trees, we can see a long way. Diamond Lake is far below us. And there are snow-covered mountain peaks all around. It's pretty awesome.

Elton sets up his camera. It's a lot bigger than mine.

He takes some establishing shots.

"What are establishing shots?" I ask him.

"Well, usually they're wide shots that give the viewer a feel for the place. To set the mood," he explains.

That sounds like a good idea, and I know Elton is a good cameraperson. So I take some establishing shots with the school camcorder.

Elton and Lucy and I stay near the tree line.

That's the place where the forest ends and the meadow begins.

Lucy is working on her shot list, so she can tell Dad and Elton what pictures she wants to be part of the show.

Wally and Dad are setting up a behavioral blind.

That means they hang around and act like they aren't interested in the hoary marmots at all, so the marmots can get used to them. In fact, Dad and Wally are acting like marmots. Dad is on his knees, smelling the grass. Ranger Wally is making digging motions with his hands.

They both keep their eyes down, so the hoary marmots won't be scared of them.

Sometimes they have to do this for an hour or two, or more.

My dad really gets into it. Now he's making loud chewing noises and scratching himself.

Lucy, the producer, reminds me that it can

take a whole day of waiting just to get a few good minutes of film! Working with animals takes a lot of patience.

I wander around and look at stuff.

I check my camcorder to make sure it's working OK.

I watch Dad and Wally act like marmots.

I wait.

Two hours later, Dad is still snuffling around the holes. But now some of the marmots are peeking out, watching him. And Elton is filming them.

"Good afternoon, Mrs. Marmot," Dad says softly. He keeps talking so that the marmots will get used to the sound of his voice.

"I'm not looking at you," he continues. "I'm not even interested. I'm just enjoying this tasty meadow feast. Have you tried the glacier lilies yet this season? I do declare, they're even sweeter than they were last year!"

Lucy tells me they probably won't use much

of this tape on Dad's show. The serious shooting will start tomorrow. "Still," she says, "you have to keep the camera running. You never know when something good will happen."

Suddenly, Elton shouts, *"Yow!"* and charges across the meadow.

Startled, the hoary marmots zip back into their burrows.

Lucy rushes to the camera and starts filming Elton as he runs in circles.

"Good!" she calls to him. "We might be able to use this!"

Elton is leaping around and brushing the back of his neck. "It bit me!" he shouts.

Usually, on a program like *The Danger Joe Show*, you don't see the cameraperson or anyone else who works behind the scenes. But every once in a while they include a shot of Elton running away from something or stepping in stuff.

Jane and I like it when that happens.

Later, I ask Elton if I can see his bite.

He shows me the red mark on the back of his neck. Lucy looks at it, too.

"Hmm," she says. "Looks like you backed into a prickly twig. I think you'll live."

It's getting late — almost time to head back down to camp. And all I've got on tape is some mountain scenery. Filming wildlife is hard work.

Oh, well. I still have most of tomorrow.

CHAPTER SEVEN
A NOISE IN THE BUSHES

It's Sunday morning.

It's cold, and my eyes don't want to stay open.

(It's not that easy sleeping in a tent. The ground is hard, even through your sleeping pad. And you keep hearing things snuffling around outside the tent.)

Also, I'm having trouble unbending my knees. Probably from too much mountain hiking yesterday.

I can tell by looking at him that Elton is having the same problem.

But after breakfast we start hiking, and my leg muscles loosen up.

Pretty soon, I feel great! I'm ready to make an awesome video.

We reach the site, and Dad tells me to keep out of the way. So I go behind a big rock with my binoculars and the camcorder.

I scan the mountainside with the binoculars.

I see a mountain goat way up near the peak. I wonder if mountain goats ever fall off the sides of mountains. I wish I had a big telephoto lens like Elton does.

I listen to my dad speaking in his television voice.

"HI! I'M DANGER JOE, AND HERE WE ARE IN THE MOSQUITO MOUNTAINS, HOT ON THE TRAIL OF SOME HOARY MARMOTS, THE LARGEST MEMBERS OF THE SQUIRREL FAMILY!

"SO, HOW DO YOU FIND A HOARY MARMOT? YOU THINK LIKE A HOARY MARMOT! THAT'S HOW!"

I told you my dad loves to say that.

"SEE THOSE ROCKS?" he continues. "THAT'S AN IDEAL PLACE FOR MARMOTS TO DIG THEIR UNDERGROUND BURROWS! THEY CAN SLEEP ALL WINTER. THEN, WHEN IT GETS WARM, THEY CAN COME OUT AND FEED ON ALL THE TASTY PLANTS IN THIS BEAUTIFUL MEADOW!"

His voice goes on and on.

I see a little head poking out from behind a nearby rock. It's a hoary marmot!

I don't move.

The marmot looks at me. He wiggles his nose and makes a snuffling noise.

I snuffle back.

"Squeak, urk, snuffle, snuffle," says the marmot.

"Urk, urk, snuffle, squeak, squeak," I reply.

"HARK! HEAR THAT?"

It sounds like my dad is getting really close. I hope he doesn't scare my marmot.

"HEAR THAT SNUFFLING NOISE?" Dad is saying in a loud whisper. "I THINK WE'VE

FOUND OURSELVES A MARMOT, AND IT'S
RIGHT BEHIND THIS ROCK!"

Dad's head appears over my rock, with Elton
and the camera right behind him.

Then Dad snaps back in surprise. Elton says,
"Oof!"

"WOOPS! IT'S ONLY JOE, JR. CUT! CUT!
Ha-ha! Good one, Joe. I knew it was you all
along!"

"But Dad!" I say. "It was a hoary marmot!" I point to the marmot.

Of course, it isn't there anymore.

"OK, that's enough fooling around. We're on a job here, Joe!"

"I wasn't . . ." I try to explain.

"Shhh . . . Don't disturb them." Dad points to the burrows.

I take my camcorder back to the tree line.

Dad continues trying to find the hoary marmots.

Finally, I grab my backpack and the camcorder and go into the spruce trees. I need a little more excitement than this. I've got a video to make!

I follow a little trail that goes down to a stream.

I hear something.

I stop and listen.

Something is moving around in the bushes ahead of me!

I get my camcorder ready.

I wait. I don't make a sound.

I see the bushes move again. It's something big! I start filming.

Something is coming through the bushes!

And then I get a great shot of Iris, the brown-haired Junior Ranger. Phooey.

Or as she would probably say, "*Poo*-ey."

And I wasn't going to have any people in my film!

"Look what I found, Miss Oliver!" Iris calls out. "It's the boy researcher!"

Miss Oliver appears, followed by the other Junior Rangers.

I think, *Why aren't they wearing their bear bells? Then I could have gotten out of the way!*

The girls crowd around and blast me with questions.

"Can I see your camcorder?"

"What's this? Hey, it's a foldout view-screen!"

"Where are your friends?"

"What's your name?"

I try to sort out the questions and get a word in.

Finally, I manage to say, "My name is Joe Denim, Jr."

"Joe Denim!" Iris says. "I've heard that name before. Hey, Justine, isn't that the name of . . . ?"

"DANGER JOE!" shouts a red-haired girl. "Joe Denim is Danger Joe's real name!"

Oh, no! What have I done?!

"We *love* Danger Joe!" they shout. "It's our favorite show! Is Danger Joe your *father*?"

I say, "No, not really. I was just kidding."

They don't even listen to me.

"I knew they were filming something!" one says. "We should have guessed it would be a wildlife show!"

Even Miss Oliver looks excited. She comes up to me. "Where are they filming, Joe?" she asks. She's looking all around, expecting to see the film crew. She thinks I'm going to tell her just because she's an adult.

"Uh . . ." I try to think fast. I can't tell them where Dad *really* is! It would ruin the shot.

"They . . . they're looking for a . . . um . . . a varied thrush! Dad heard one singing in the cedar forest. Down there." I point down the mountain. "They're looking for it now. I . . . uh . . . had to get out of the way, so I came up here."

Miss Oliver gives me a shrewd look and says, "Yes. I am familiar with the varied thrush. Come along, girls. This is the chance of a lifetime!" They start down the trail.

"Wait!" I say. "You can't go down there! You'll scare the birds!"

"Don't worry, Joe, Jr.," Iris says. "We're Junior Rangers! We can be *very* quiet."

They're gone. Whew! I guess I fooled them, all right!

I wait quietly until I'm sure they're gone, and then I turn back toward the site.

And that's when I see it.

About a hundred yards upstream, just ambling along, big and furry and brown with a hump on its back — it's a GRIZZLY!

CHAPTER EIGHT
GRIZZLY!

Wow! Or, as my dad would say, GREAT GALLOPING GECKOS!

This is the best!

The bear stops and stands up. That's what they do when they smell or hear something and they want to check it out.

I look around for a tree in case I need to start climbing, but the bear isn't looking my way.

I check the wind. Uh-oh. I'm downwind of the bear. That means he can't smell me and get out of my way! The only thing I can do is hope he doesn't see me! I guess I might as well shoot some film, as long as he's there.

Grizzlies have an incredible sense of smell. My dad says they can smell *a lot* better than dogs, and I know that dogs can smell about a million times better than humans!

A bear's sense of hearing is much better than ours, too.

I lift the camcorder slowly and carefully.

I wait until the bear is rustling the bushes before I start filming, because the camcorder *whirrs* a little bit.

Oh, boy! This is going to be great!

The bear is sniffing the air.

Then he starts to follow his nose.

And I follow him. I stay well back, and I use the zoom lens.

The bear climbs over a big rock. He stops and stares.

I wonder what he's looking at. When he continues, I climb up and peek over the rock, so I can see what the bear can see.

Uh-oh. I should have known!

It's Danger Joe.

Dad is holding a microphone in front of a hoary marmot's nose. The hoary marmot is not afraid of him.

Suddenly the marmot gives her loud, piercing warning cry.

"HEAR THAT?" says Danger Joe, looking toward the camera. "THAT'S THE WARNING CRY OF THE HOARY MARMOT," he says. "SHE'S SEEN OR HEARD OR SMELLED SOMETHING. SHE'S WAITING TO FIND OUT IF IT'S A REAL THREAT! IF IT IS, THEN, *ZIP*! SHE'LL DIVE RIGHT DOWN INTO HER BURROW, QUICK AS A WINK!"

Zip! The marmot disappears.

Dad doesn't notice. He's still talking toward Elton, who is filming. "THIS MARMOT HAS TO BE ON THE LOOKOUT FOR ALL KINDS OF MEAT-EATING ANIMALS. A FULL-GROWN HOARY MARMOT WOULD MAKE A NICE, GOOD-SIZED MEAL FOR A

GOLDEN EAGLE, A FOX, A WOLVERINE, OR EVEN A HUNGRY . . ."

"GRIZZLY!" shouts Elton.

The grizzly has been walking, on his hind legs, up behind Danger Joe. He must have just come into the range of Elton's viewfinder.

But Dad still doesn't see the bear. He says, "THAT'S RIGHT, ELTON. GRIZZLIES ARE ANOTHER SOURCE OF DANGER TO OUR HOARY MARMOT FRIENDS."

Elton is backing up slowly. He points and Dad turns around.

"OH-HO!" he shouts, "WHAT LUCK! HERE IS A GRIZZLY RIGHT NOW! AND HE'S A WHOPPER! WHAT A BEAUTIFUL ANIMAL! HEAR THAT?" Dad holds the mike up to the bear's mouth. "*CLACK, CLACK.* HE'S CLACKING HIS TEETH, WARNING ME TO WATCH OUT. TAKE A LOOK AT THOSE TEETH, TOO. NICE AND SHARP!"

The grizzly goes *grrrrr* and shows his teeth to my dad.

What will the grizzly do next?

Will my dad be okay?

Then there's another loud squeal. Only this time it isn't a hoary marmot.

"Ooh! There he is! It's Danger Joe!"

Oh, no! It's those Junior Rangers! They must have circled through the forest and come back!

How sneaky can you get?! I'll bet they knew all along that I was trying to trick them!

They're pointing at Dad and squealing. They don't even see the grizzly bear. (You'd think Junior Rangers would notice a little thing like that!)

Lucy, the producer, and Ranger Wally are trying to get their attention. I can see Lucy pointing at the bear.

But Dad is only interested in the grizzly. He's still talking to the camera. "NOW THIS

BEAR IS GETTING MAD. SEE HOW HE FLATTENS HIS EARS? THAT'S NOT A HAPPY SIGN. PRETTY SOON THIS FINE GRIZZLY WILL GET DOWN ON ALL FOURS, AND THEN, WATCH OUT!"

CHAPTER NINE
JOE, JR., TO THE RESCUE

Dad's right. The grizzly is mad!

Here's the situation:

Dad is on one side of the grizzly.

I'm on the other side, hidden behind a bush.

The bear hasn't seen me yet.

All the others — Lucy, Ranger Wally, and the Junior Rangers — are down by the trees. Except Elton.

Elton is still filming.

Elton might complain a lot. But when he gets involved in shooting an exciting scene, he can be a real hero!

The girls have seen the bear now, and they're

being quiet. They are crowded together behind Wally and Lucy and the two grown-up leaders. They're standing their ground but not making eye contact. Good. The bear might not want to risk attacking such a big group.

GRRRRRRR.

The grizzly glares at them.

They stand firm.

He drops down on all fours and takes a few leaps in their direction.

Then he lets out a huge ***GGRRRROWWWL!*** and rushes right at them!

Yow!

I don't know about those girls, but I almost pee in my pants! Luckily, I don't. I just drop everything and run about ten feet farther into the bushes.

But the grizzly stops after a couple of leaps. He blows through his nose.

Dad says, "WOO-HOO! DID YOU SEE

THAT BIG GUY RUN! Are you getting this, Elton?"

Then the bear turns and gives Dad a look. He snorts again.

Uh-oh. Dad never knows when it's time to start thinking about his own safety! I guess it's up to me. I have to get that bear away from my dad!

It's time for me to start to . . . THINK LIKE A GRIZZLY!

OK, OK. Let's see. If I were a grizzly, I'd be thinking, *I'm mad, because these humans have invaded my space. Why didn't they wear their stupid bear bells? Then I could have gotten out of their way!* And I'd be thinking, *Now I feel trapped. And I don't like it! I wish they would all go away and leave the mountain to me and the marmots!*

The marmots! Now there's an idea.

Maybe, if I make noises like a hoary marmot, I can distract the bear.

"SCREEEEEEEECH!" I whistle.

The grizzly wheels away from Dad and looks at me.

Oops. Maybe that wasn't such a good idea. Even though I've moved way back behind the bushes, I don't like the way the bear is looking at me.

Then I hear another *SCREEEECH!* from partway up the mountain.

Then another and another!

The marmots are passing on my warning!

The grizzly snorts and stands up on his back legs. He's looking at the marmots as they poke their heads up out of their holes. He looks pretty interested.

He starts to leap toward one of their holes but then stops short, right in front of my bush. In fact, right near where I was hiding before. Whew, it's a good thing I moved!

He growls. He pounces. And when he rears

up, he's holding the school camcorder in his huge paws!

Oh, no! I must have dropped it when I ran to hide! The camera is still running. I can hear the whirring noise.

GRRAAGH! The grizzly opens his jaws and clamps his teeth down on the camcorder.

C-R-U-N-C-H!

He shakes his head wildly back and forth, then spits the camcorder out, gives it a disgusted look, and lopes off up the mountain.

The hoary marmots are all quiet now, safe inside their burrows.

And Dad is talking to Elton's camera again. "WHAT A MAGNIFICENT, TOTALLY UN-PREDICTABLE

ANIMAL! THAT'S WHAT MAKES EVERY ENCOUNTER WITH A GRIZZLY BEAR SO FASCINATING!

"WHAT DO I ALWAYS TELL YOU? NOTHING IS MORE AMAZING THAN NATURE!

"AND THAT'S THE TRUTH!"

CHAPTER TEN
BACK IN SCHOOL

Back in school, I finish my story. "So that's how the camcorder got wrecked."

The kids are all looking at me with their mouths hanging open.

"But don't worry," I say. "Elton says he can save my video! The only thing is, I can't show it today, because they want to use one of the shots on *The Danger Joe Show* — the one where the grizzly's jaws are biting down on the camera lens."

"What about the Junior Rangers?" Tara Bean asks me.

"Oh. Well, they were all OK," I say. "They went running up to my dad, yelling, 'You saved us!' Then he had to autograph their hats."

Edgar Pitts snorts.

"No," says Tara, "I mean, like, how old were they? And where do they live? And how do you join their club?"

"Yeah," says Larry Reed, "and are they only girls? Or can boys be Junior Rangers, too?"

I don't know the answers to these questions.

Mrs. Wright says she will try to find out. And that reminds me of something else.

"And Mrs. Wright?" I say, "My dad says to tell you that *The Danger Joe Show* will buy a new camcorder for the school. And do we want the one that's five pounds and has a shoulder rest or the one-pound, pocket-sized model?"

Mrs. Wright says she'll look into it and let my dad know. And she says, "Thank you for your exciting story, Joe. We all look forward to seeing your video when it's ready."

I smile and nod my head at Mrs. Wright. Then I sit down next to Bernie and Kay. And the kids start clapping.

I guess they don't hate me anymore.
All except for Edgar Pitts, of course.
Well, that's OK. I'm used to that.
I stand up and take a bow.

THE GRIZZLY BEAR

George D. Lepp / Photo Researchers, Inc.

GRIZZLY BEARS are also called BROWN BEARS.

The actual color of their fur can be anything from tan to almost black. The name GRIZZLY comes from the fact that their fur is often "grizzled" — that is, tipped with white.

The grizzled fur is one of the grizzly's distinguishing characteristics. Distinguishing characteristics are ways to tell grizzlies from other bears. Another distinguishing characteristic is the big hump over a grizzly's shoulders. This hump is really an enormous mass of powerful digging muscle.

In North America, brown (or grizzly) bears live from Arctic Canada to Alaska to protected areas in the mountains of Wyoming.

They are fast and strong and can eat almost anything. A good part of their diet is plant foods, like roots and grasses and berries. Along the shore, they dig up clams and eat barnacles off rocks. They will hunt and eat all kinds of animals, from ants to fish to caribou. They will also eat the old meat of animals they find already dead.

Full-grown grizzlies are six to ten feet tall when standing on their hind legs, and usually weigh up to about 600 pounds. But in some areas, where there is plenty of food, they can weigh over one ton!

Picture a grizzly bear's feet. They are big and flat. The soles are heavily padded and covered with thick, tough leather. The front claws are four to six inches long and made for digging.

With these feet, a grizzly can travel all day and night over rough ground. But it can also walk on top of deep snow without sinking in, strip small berries from a bush, open up clams, and unscrew the lids of jars. A grizzly can also dig a six-foot tunnel in a mountainside.

Grizzlies have excellent memories and good eyesight. And they can hear and smell much, much better than humans.

Another amazing thing about grizzly bears is the way they sleep through the winter.

After fattening up in the fall, a grizzly will dig a tunnel. Maybe it will be under the roots of a big tree, or deep inside a snowbank. At the end of the tunnel, there will be a small bedroom, or den. The floor of this den will be covered with three to fourteen inches of spruce and fir boughs, or soft grasses and moss. The grizzly will climb inside and sleep for up to seven months without eating, without drinking, and without eliminating waste.

Now, *that's* amazing!

DANGER JOE'S CREATURE FEATURE
THE HOARY MARMOT

S. J. Krasemann/Peter Arnold, Inc.

HOARY MARMOTS are close relatives of woodchucks and are the largest members of the squirrel family. The word "hoary" refers to the icy gray coloring of their fur.

Hoary marmots are often heard before they are seen, making loud, long whistles whenever they sense danger. This alarm cry warns all the small mammals in the area to take cover.

Hoary marmots live in northwestern North America, high up on south-facing mountainsides, where they dig their burrows among the large protective rocks. During the long, cold winters they sleep curled up inside their burrows. In warm weather they come out to feed on mountain meadow plants, lie around in the sun, and play. But if it gets too hot, back they go, into the burrows, where it's cool, and dark, and free of mosquitoes.

DANGER JOE'S WILD WORDS

BEHAVIORAL BLIND: A blind is a place where someone hides while watching wildlife. In a behavioral blind you "hide" behind your behavior. You act peaceful and nonthreatening until the animal becomes used to you.

BLACK BEARS: Despite their name, black bears are not always black. They can be light brown or dark brown, sometimes silver, and — rarely — even white! They are smaller than grizzly bears, live in forested areas, and are expert tree climbers.

BLACK RACER: Racers are long, slender, evenly colored snakes that are common throughout much of the United States. Their color varies from greenish brown to blue-black. In the wild, the black racer is usually found in the East.

BULL SNAKE: Bull snakes are large (forty-eight to a hundred inches long) constrictor-type snakes with black or brown blotches on their backs and sides. A constrictor kills its prey by squeezing it until the prey cannot breathe.

FLOATPLANE: A floatplane is a special kind of aircraft with floats, or pontoons, for landing on water.

GLACIER LILIES: Glacier lilies are one of the first flowers to come up and bloom after the snow in the mountains has melted. Their beautiful yellow blossoms hang down, facing the ground, and their bulbs are a favorite food of grizzly bears.

IGUANA: The common, or green, iguana is a large lizard that is found in the forests of tropical Central and South America.

MIGRATING: Migrating means moving. Animals often migrate with the change of the seasons.

MOUNTAIN GOAT: The mountain goat is a shaggy white goat that lives on the highest mountain ledges. Mountain goats *do* sometimes lose their balance and fall.

MOUNTAIN LION: Mountain lions are the biggest kind of wildcat in North America; a mountain lion is also called a COUGAR, PUMA, or PANTHER.

NATURAL HABITAT: An animal's natural habitat is the place, or type of area, where it normally lives.

PAINTED TURTLE: The painted turtle is common in North America. It has a smooth, dark shell that is usually edged with red marks. The turtle's underside can be light yellow to red, plain or patterned. Its head and legs are striped with yellow and red.

RATTLESNAKE: The rattlesnake is a deadly poisonous snake with horny beads, or rattles, on the tip of its tail. When the rattler shakes its tail, the rattles make a warning, buzzing sound. There are at least sixteen different kinds of rattlesnakes in North America.

SCAT: Scat is a word scientists use for animal droppings, or . . . poo.

TELEPHOTO LENS: This is a camera lens that makes distant subjects appear large.

VARIED THRUSH: This bird is orange and gray. It is found in northwestern forests of North America.

VENOM: Venom is a type of poison. Animals use venom to protect themselves and to kill other animals for food. Animals that use venom are *venomous*.

ABOUT THE AUTHOR AND ILLUSTRATOR

Jon Buller does more of the illustrating, and Susan Schade does more of the writing, but they both do some of each. Altogether, they have published over forty books, including *20,000 Baseball Cards Under the Sea* and *Space Dog Jack*. They are married and live in Lyme, Connecticut, where they can often be found walking in the local forests, looking for mushrooms, and paddling kayaks in local rivers and streams. They used to have two pet snails, but they decided to release them back into their natural habitat.